Mrs. Fitch

DATE DUE			

E
KET

3 4880 00030764 0
Ketteman, Helen.

The Christmas
blizzard

the Christmas Blizzard

the Christmas Blizzard

By Helen Ketteman

Illustrated by James Warhola

SCHOLASTIC INC.
New York   Toronto   London   Auckland   Sydney
Mexico City   New Delhi   Hong Kong

ISBN 0-590-13609-7

12 11 10 9 8 7 6 5 4 3 2 1   9/9 0 1 2 3 4/0

Printed in the U.S.A.   14

First Scholastic Trade paperback printing, November 1999

The illustrations in this book were executed in watercolor and ink
on Arches watercolor paper.

To William and
Dorothy Tye
— H.K.

To Katy, Abby,
and Donny
— J.W.

Little Sissy McNab ran up to Maynard Jenkins when he came into the McNab General Store.

"Mr. Jenkins, Mr. Jenkins!" she cried. "The weatherman says we're going to get a blizzard tonight!"

"Hmmphff!" said the old man. "That whippersnapper of a weatherman wouldn't know a blizzard if it tipped its hat and introduced itself. The blizzard of '22 — now THAT was a blizzard to remember!"

"How much did it snow?" Sissy asked.

The old man settled on a chair and warmed his hands over the stove. "Don't be so all-fired anxious, girl," he replied. "Learning history takes time.

"That year, the weather was crazy. It was so cold that when my pappy dropped his sledgehammer, it shattered like glass. The ground cracked, too, and pretty deep. Ellie Cogwell said she could see clear through to China. 'Course, Ellie always was one for exaggerating.

The weather was afflicting other places, too. Up at the North Pole, why, it was as warm as grandma's gravy. Palm trees were sprouting right and left. It was so hot, Santa's elves weren't in the mood to make toys.

So Santa packed up and moved his whole workshop, elves, reindeer, and all. He looked for the coldest spot in the world and ended up settling right here. Said it felt more like the North Pole than the North Pole did.

Turned out, we almost missed Christmas that year. Cold as it was, it had been as dry as cornshucks since August. Not a cloud in the sky for months. No rain. No sleet. No snow. Not a flake.

One day in October, I slipped by Santa's place. I peeked in the window to see if he was making that shiny red sled I wanted. But Santa and his elves weren't doing a thing. Turned out, the elves needed more than cold weather to make toys for Christmas. They needed snow, and plenty of it.

I looked up at the sky and what did I see but blue. If we were going to have Christmas at all, I knew I had to do something, and quick.

I went to a shack outside of town, over by Hatcher's Pond, where old Miz Pendersnarf lived. It was rumored she could cast spells. I knocked, and the door creaked open.

Miz Pendersnarf seemed old enough to be Santa's granny. Her hair was piled up like a rat's nest, and she was so squinty-eyed, I couldn't tell for sure if she had eyeballs or not. She looked awful scary. 'What is it, boy?' she croaked.

I gathered my courage and told her why we needed snow. Miz Pendersnarf agreed to help. She pulled bottles of dried herbs off the shelf and stirred them together in a bowl. She lit a match, and the herbs flared up, then fizzled and smoked. Miz Pendersnarf smiled a snaggle-toothed grin.

'There's gon' be a wind,' she said, 'a strong, strong wind. That's all you need, boy. Nature will do the rest.'

I was halfway home when the wind whipped up. Whoo-ee! Did that spell work great! It lifted me and blew me all the rest of the way.

That night, the wind howled and whistled. Got stronger by the hour. By morning, frozen trees had been shattered into firewood and blown into stacks. By afternoon, rain clouds had swept in all the way from Seattle, Washington. And then, as suddenly as the wind had begun, it stopped.

Those Seattle clouds were bursting with moisture. I figured it would start snowing right away. Santa and his elves must have thought so, too, 'cause they perked up and started cranking out the toys.

But Nature wasn't through with us yet. Those clouds looked heavy, but they didn't do a blessed thing.

Later, in the dead of night, I heard a loud crash. Felt just like an earthquake and threw me out of bed. And the racket! Sounded louder than one of those new-fangled jet aeroplanes.

Come to find out, those clouds had froze solid. Crashed right to the ground. One of them even squashed the roof of Jed McDonald's barn. It exploded, scattering cows as far as four miles away, and some up in trees, to boot. Jed sure had a hard time collecting those cows.

You should have seen this town, girl. Dark, lumpy, frozen clouds were lying all over the ground! And they were as slippery as a weasel in a grease pit, too. It was so slippery, Santa's reindeer wouldn't be able to get off the ground to deliver toys. I had work to do.

I decided to force those clouds back up in the sky, so I slid all over town lighting bonfires with the frozen, stacked firewood. Everyone pitched in and helped.

Wasn't long before those clouds started thawing out, and when they did, they rose back up in the sky where they belonged. We kept the fires going 'round the clock 'til it finally got warm enough to snow.

And by George, it snowed like there was no tomorrow. Flakes as big as dinner plates. Flakes as fat as turnips. Flakes rounder than a Thanksgiving turkey. Flakes fluffier than a long-haired barn cat. Why, those Seattle clouds snowed up a blizzard for two whole weeks!

By the time the storm had ended, the houses were all covered. The doors were snowed shut, so we climbed out the chimney and started shoveling.

We finished two days later, just in time to see the elves load Santa's sleigh on Christmas Eve. Those elves must have worked overtime, because I never did see so many toys.

On Christmas morning, I woke up, and there, under my Christmas tree, was the red sled I'd asked for. Old Miz Pendersnarf got a sled, too, and we had fine times racing down Dead Man's Hill. We sledded all spring and into the summer. Miz Pendersnarf was one bodacious sledder!

It was because of her that the town got its new name. We had voted to change it from Waterville to Blizzard, because of the storm. On Founder's Day, Mayor Butterfrump was making the dedication speech when Miz Pendersnarf came barreling down Dead Man's Hill. She crashed through the fancy new sign, smashing the 'B' in Blizzard to smithereens. The mayor stayed cool as ice cream. Without blinking an eye, Mayor Butterfrump shouted, 'Welcome to *Lizzard*, Indiana.' And that's been the name ever since."

Maynard winked at Sissy. "I reckon you've learned enough history for one day, girl. I'm goin' home to dust off my old sled and oil it up. If we get that pinch of snow your weatherman predicts, I might just test it out."

Maynard waved as he disappeared out the door. "See you tomorrow, Sissy. Up on Dead Man's Hill."